Charlie and the Scavenger Hunt

Dyslexic Friendly Edition

TIF E. BOOTS

Illustrated by Syranity Barker

DF Version ISBN-13: 978-1-963272-27-7

ShelteringTree.Earth, LLC
PO Box 973, Eagle Lake, FL 33839

ShelteringTreeMedia.com

What is a "Dyslexic Friendly" Book?

Sheltering Tree Media has taken steps to make our books more friendly for those who live with dyslexia. While the following principles will not make every book readable for every reader, it is our best effort to create products that encourage reading and to support all readers.

Throughout the book, we use a font named OpenDyslexic. This is a free font that is designed to help dyslexic readers distinguish each letter from the others. For more information about OpenDyslexic, how it differs from other fonts, and research behind the font, visit their website: www.opendyslexic.com.

In our books created for children, we use a font size which provides the reader with plenty of spacing between the letters (which is called kerning). The bigger, wider font tends to be easier to the reader's eyes.

The space between each word is increased (this is called word spacing). This helps better to distinguish when one word ends and the next begins. The line spacing is greater than most common fonts (this is called *leading*). This all should help with readability.

Whenever possible, the text is Left-Aligned but it is not justified on the right side. Allowing the right side of a paragraph to remain *rough* keeps the word spacing consistent throughout.

Our Dyslexic Friendly books are printed on cream or ivory paper which is also thicker than the average book page. This minimizes the sharp contrast of black-on-white pages as well as bleedthrough of text from the previous page.

Finally, Sheltering Tree Media has made colored overlays available when you purchase a book through our online store. You can find these overlays at ShelteringTreeMedia.com/shop/dyslexic-friendly.

These are some of the principles we use to create a book as readable as possible to those living with dyslexia. Some may find this helpful; some may not. Please provide us with any insights you might have to improve our Dyslexic Friendly principles. We pray this will enable many to heighten their love for reading.

DEDICATION

For Clarice who is my sounding board, my
marketer, my inspiration and who thinks
she is my editor.

CHARLIE and the SCAVENGER HUNT

Brutus ran to Scrump's tree. It was a beautiful cool morning, and he was eager to play with his best friends.

"Scrump," he called, "come out and play. I have an idea for a fun adventure."

Scrump poked his head out of his hole and looked around. "Good morning, Brutus. Have you already found Charlie?"

"I'm here," chattered Charlie from above. "Brutus sounded so excited, I had to come see why."

"I think we should have a scavenger hunt today," blurted Brutus, unable to contain his excitement.

"Oh, that would be so much fun!" agreed Scrump.

"We could go all over the farm," said Charlie. "But what would we be looking for?

"I have some ideas." said Brutus. "We could find things of different colors. Like a black horsehair, and an orange leaf, since the trees are changing colors. I think we need more than two things to find though."

"Are we looking as a team or alone as a contest?" asked Scrump.

"I think it would be fun as a team but more of a challenge as a contest," said Charlie. "We could each bring the items back here one at a time as we find them and whoever finds them all the fastest is the winner."

"Ok," agreed Brutus. "What else should we try to find?"

The Friends thought and each came up with different things to find. All of the things were of different colors. A black horsehair, an orange leaf, a golden stalk of wheat, a purple flower, something white, a brown pinecone, something blue, a red fruit, and a green plant. Once they had all decided what to find, they each ran in a different direction.

Brutus went the horse pasture first. Along the wooden fence he found a long black horsehair. He ran back to the tree with it and started a pile of his finds. Then he ran around the house to the driveway. The whole driveway was made with white rocks. On his way back to the tree, he saw brown pinecone and stopped to pick it up.

"Wait," he heard a voice from the tree above him.

Brutus looked up to find Twitter looking down at him. "Hi Twitter, I'm sorry I can't really talk right now. We are having a scavenger hunt, and whoever finds everything the fastest is the winner!"

"I know," said Twitter. "I was nearby when you were making the rules. I think you forgot about bringing the stuff back to the tree one at a time."

14

"You're right," Brutus agreed. "I was so excited about finding stuff that I forgot to take the rock back first. I am not even sure why we made a rule to take things back one at a time."

"I do not know why that rule came up," agreed Twitter. "But I do think it is a good one. You are so much bigger than Charlie and Scrump. You could take advantage of your size and carry several things at once. Or you could find a bucket and carry everything at once. You would be done before they even got the first three things back to the tree."

"That would definitely make me the winner!" exclaimed Brutus. "But you're right, it would not be very fair and it would take away the fun for everyone. It is a good rule."

"Take your rock back to the tree and come back for the pinecone," instructed Twitter. "You have wasted time talking to me. Now they will have a head start."

"That's okay," said Brutus. "Whatever time I've lost was worth it to talk to a friend."

Scrump ran to the clover field and pulled up a green clover plant. Brutus and Scrump returned to the tree at the same time. They put their prizes in separate piles. They did not see Charlie, just a patch of grass sitting on the root of the tree. They looked at each other and shrugged, then ran away to find the next thing.

Scrump ran to the barn. He found a black horsehair on a brush. He ran back to put the hair on his pile then ran through the clover field to the wheat field. "It's a good thing we have so many fields," he thought to himself.

Charlie ran through the yard to the garden. He quickly found a purple flower and a red strawberry but could not carry them both at the same time. While he thought of a solution he looked around, next to a bush he saw a blue feather. Now he had three things to take back to the tree but how could he do it all in one trip?

"You look confused," a voice said from the bushes. Charlie jumped and Patches the Skunk stepped out of the shadows.

"Hi, Patches, you scared me," laughed Charlie. "We are having a scavenger hunt. I found three of the things but do not know how to get them all back to my pile in one trip."

Patches thought for a moment, "I saw some string by the garden tools. Maybe I can tie the stuff to your back," she suggested.

"That might work," said Charlie.

Patches turned around to go find the string, "Wait a minute," she exclaimed. "Is it cheating for me to help you?"

"Oh," Charlie thought back to when they were making up the rules. "I think it might be. We are supposed to take things back to the tree one at a time. Nothing was said about having help to carry them, but we did decide not to work with teams this time."

"That sounds like you are each supposed to do this alone," said Patches. "But I do not think it would be cheating if I were to stay here with two of the things you have already found, so they do not get lost while you are taking the other to your pile."

"That would be great," said Charlie. "Thank you so much."

Scrump had already put the green plant, black horsehair, and golden wheat in his pile. He returned to the tree again with a white piece of shell that he found by the pond, then ran as fast as he could to the edge of the woods. He quickly found a pinecone and picked it up. While heading back towards the tree, he looked for an orange leaf.

Scrump did not see any orange leaves on the ground anywhere. He put the pinecone in his pile and ran back to the woods. Looking down for a leaf while bouncing along, he ran directly into Lawrence the fox.

"Ouch," Lawrence exclaimed while rubbing his nose. "What are you doing?"

"I'm so sorry, Lawrence, I'm afraid I was not watching where I was going." Scrump continued, "We are having a scavenger hunt. I was too focused on finding an orange leaf to watch where I was going."

"Well, leaves are usually in the trees, not on the ground," stated Lawrence. "Do you want me to see if someone can fly up there and get one for you?"

"No, but thanks for the offer," Scrump declined. "We decided not to work with teams, and I think having someone get it for me could be cheating."

"I see your point," said Lawrence. "But the leaves back here have not started to fall yet. You may not be able to find one on the ground."

"Oh no," whined Scrump. "I thought the leaf would be the easiest one to find."

"Well," Lawrence thought out loud. "If leaves are changing colors in the trees, they should be changing colors in the bushes, too."

"What a great idea!" exclaimed Scrump. "I never thought about looking at other plants with leaves. Thank you so much."

It didn't take long for Scrump to find his leaf once he started looking in the right places.

Charlie scurried back to the tree to add his blue feather to the pile. The feather was the last item on his list. He looked at his pile. It now had a black horsehair, an orange leaf, a purple flower, a red strawberry the blue feather, and a green plant. There was a brown pinecone, a white rock, and a golden piece of wheat. He had everything!

Scrump came hopping back to the tree carrying a red cherry. In his pile, Charlie saw the black horsehair, orange leaf, golden wheat, a green clover, the brown pinecone, and a purple lilac. Scrump also had a white piece of shell and a blue bit of ribbon. With the red cherry Scrump added, his pile was complete.

Brutus came running up to them after dropping a fat blueberry into his pile. He looked over at them with a frown. "Have you both found everything?" He hoped that his friends were not done with the hunt yet.

"Yes," replied Scrump. "Charlie was here first with his last find. I guess that means he won."

"But I wanted to win."
Brutus whined, "I knew I
should have brought back
the pinecone and the rock at
the same time. I would have
been done faster."

"The rules we decided on
were fair and said to bring
everything one at a time. If
you would have done that, it
would have been cheating,
and the win would not have
been an honest win,"
Scrump's foot thumped with
each point.

"Patches was going to help me by tying three things onto me so I could bring them all back in one trip," Charlie told them. "But since the rule was one thing for each trip, it did not feel right. I think if I had done that and then won, I would not feel like I deserved the win."

"I worked really hard and ran really fast," Brutus complained. "I should have made less trips and carried more at once. I would have won."

Charlie and Scrump looked at each other. Brutus had never acted like this before.

"Brutus," said Scrump. "Is winning by cheating your friends really winning?"

"I don't think it is," answered Charlie. "Everyone worked hard but everyone cannot win and no one wins if someone cheats. Cheating makes the game no fun for everyone that is playing."

"I see what you guys mean," Brutus pouted. "We all had a chance to cheat. If we had all cheated, it may have hurt each other and our friendship. Next time I will just have to work harder and be faster. It's okay not to win if you have fun and try your best."

"Yes," agreed Scrump. "There is always another game. Not winning this one doesn't mean you won't win tomorrow's. By not being a bad loser, you are still a winner. You had fun spending time with your friends."

"Speaking of friends," Brutus grinned. "How about we get everyone together for a relay race tomorrow? We can work as teams with Patches, Lawrence, Twitter, and Dash."

"That sounds exciting," Scrump agreed.

"It sure does," chittered Charlie just as his sister Colleen ran down the tree.

"Mom says it's time to come in," she told him.

"Ok," said Charlie. He turned to his friends, "Good night, guys. I'll see you tomorrow."

Charlie and his sister scampered up the tree. Brutus turned to walk away, and Scrump dove back into his rabbit hole just as his mom tried to poke her head out to call for him.

ABOUT THE AUTHOR

Tif E. Boots wrote her first children's book as a birthday present for her daughter. Many years later it has been shared with her sister, cousins, classmates, and now you.

Tif was raised in Marana, Arizona and was working concession stands at county fairs in Arizona and Michigan with her family until she graduated from Marana High School in 2000. She became a mother and correctional officer in 2004. She then moved to Nevada, Missouri with her family where she was blessed with her second daughter and fell into a career of nurse's assistant for Hospice.

Tif and her family relocated to Mulberry, Florida in 2017. In her free time, Tif can usually be found on the water or at amusement parks spending time with family and friends, and simply enjoying the life that God has blessed her with.

ABOUT THE ILLUSTRATOR

Syranity Barker is an illustrator who has always had a love for art. She was born in Tucson, Arizona and eventually moved to central Florida where she graduated high school.

Syranity illustrated her love of drawing early in life; her family were great supporters of her passions and always made sure she had a variety of supplies and mediums. While she was still in high school, her work was entered in numerous art shows. She received the *City Commissioners Choice Award* for a mixed media portrait of her dog and has sold several pieces of her work.

Still fresh out of high school, Syranity works two jobs and illustrates professionally in her spare time. She is currently the in-house illustrator for *Sheltering Tree.Earth Publishing* and also promotes herself as a free-lance artist.

Syranity enjoys singing, skating, spending time with her friends and family, and creating her own characters and writing backstories for them.

Syranity aspires to become an art teacher and share her passion for drawing and self-expression with others.

these Items? Good Luck! ☺

DISCUSSION GUIDE FOR SMALL GROUPS, CLASSES, AND INDIVIDUAL REFLECTION

DIRECTIONS: Write your answers on the lines. In the space below the lines, draw a picture explaining your answer.

1. Why is Brutus eager to play with his friends?

_____

_____

_____

_____

2. What is Brutus's idea?

_____

_____

_____

_____

3. What is a Scavenger Hunt?

_____

_____

_____

_____

4. Name 5 things they were supposed to find.

_____

_____

_____

_____

5. Where did Brutus go first? Why do you think he went there first?

_____

_____

_____

_____

6. Who did Brutus find in the front yard?

_____

_____

_____

_____

7. Do you think Brutus was trying to cheat when Twitter found him?

_____

_____

_____

_____

8. Do you think taking one thing back to the tree before finding another is a good rule?

_____

_____

_____

_____

9. What does Scrump find first?

_____

_____

_____

_____

10. Where does Charlie find a purple flower?

_____

_____

_____

_____

11. Who scares Charlie while he is thinking in the garden?

_____

_____

_____

_____

12. Do you think having help to carry stuff is cheating?

_____

_____

_____

_____

13. Who does Scrump run into while looking for a leaf?

_____

_____

_____

_____

14. Where does Lawrence suggest looking for a leaf?

_____

_____

_____

_____

15. Who got all the items to the tree first?

_____

_____

_____

_____

16. Who was second to find everything?

_____

_____

_____

_____

17. What do you think of Brutus's behavior and attitude when he didn't win?

_____

_____

_____

_____

18. Where the rules fair for everyone that was playing?

_____

_____

_____

_____

19. Would you want to keep playing games with Brutus?

_____

_____

_____

_____

20. Would cheating to win really be better than losing if you lost friends?

_____

_____

_____

_____

21. Have you ever cheated to win? How did it make you feel? How did your friends feel about it?

_____

_____

_____

_____

SHELTERING TREE

Earth
Publishing
ShelteringTreeMedia.com

For more information,
to become one of our authors,
translators, or illustrators,
or to contact the author or illustrator:

ShelteringTreeMedia.com